The Gift Your Gift

The Unexpected Blessings
of Chaos

by Dr. Ayanna Burns

with Dr. Sam Davis

The Gift Your Gift
The Unexpected Blessings of Chaos

Published by

JOYFUL SOUND MINISTRIES

Published by Joyful Sound Ministries, Inc.
©2021 by Ayanna Burns with Sam Davis
International Standard Book Number: 978-1-7354820-0-2
Cover design by Robin Raymond, LLC

For information:
JOYFUL SOUND MINISTRIES, INC.
501 GOLDEN ROD COURT
BLYTHEWOOD, SC 29016

The Unexpected Blessings of Chaos parable is a work of fiction.
Names, characters, incidents and dialogue are the product of the author's imagination or are used fictitiously.
Any resemblance to actual events, places or persons, living or dead, is coincidental.

Want to receive **FREE** information from Dr. Burns and Dr. Davis?
Click below to start receiving your free information:

Visit tgygift.com

Contents

Preface

Prologue

CHAPTER 1: Meet Chaos

CHAPTER 2: The Value of Chaos

CHAPTER 3: Getting Through Chaos

CHAPTER 4: What Makes Chaos, Chaos?

CHAPTER 5: Changing the Tides of Chaos

CHAPTER 6: From Chaos to Order

CHAPTER 7: The Hope of Chaos

Decision Time

The Unexpected Gift

SERIES

When the gift you receive is not what you expected.

ACKNOWLEDGEMENTS

A very special thanks to The Gift-Source Himself. Thank You Lord for showing me the blessings found in chaos and for sending those who dedicated their time and efforts to this book's completion including Tareon Ware.
Your insights and assistance were invaluable.

John 13:7 (NIV)

Jesus replied, "You do not realize now what I am doing,
but later you will understand."

**Blessed are those who experience chaos for they shall receive
peace, calm and order.**

Preface

"To keep me from becoming conceited and snobbish, I was given a problem and it's a thorn in my side. The thorn is quite irritating, aggravating, frustrating and oftentimes painful. Several times, I begged The Gift-Source to remove it but The Gift-Source allowed it to remain. The Gift-Source said to me, 'My grace is sufficient for you, for My power is made perfect in weakness.'

"How strange. How can it be?," I thought to myself. "How is it that I am actually empowered and strengthened when I was given something that was meant to weaken me?

"Therefore I will boast all the more gladly about my weaknesses, so that The Gift-Source's power may rest upon me."

Prologue

There is a story about Human who needed a gift. One day, Human decided to visit the house of The Gift-Source who was well-known for providing extraordinary and perfect gifts.

"I need a gift," Human humbly said to The Gift-Source.

"Do you trust me? Do you have faith in Me?," asked The Gift-Source.

"Yes I do because I know Your Son, the Savior," Human replied. "I trust you completely. I have faith in You for nothing is impossible for You."

"Very well. Since you acknowledged My Son as your Savior, you are now one of My children. As one of My children, you are hereby granted all the benefits and privileges of being in My family, including the right to talk to Me whenever you want.

"Furthermore, since you trust Me, I will give you a series of gifts instead of just one. And don't worry. You have My word. I will supply what you need. My Son will be with you, interceding for you. Since you accepted my Son, you also have a special bonus gift: The Guidance-Counselor Who will be with you.

"The Guidance-Counselor will advise and lead you and help you use your gifts properly. When we communicate with one another, The Guidance-Counselor will also relay messages to you from me and vice-versa. The Guidance-Counselor will serve as our translator of the messages. You see, the three of us (My Son, The Guidance-Counselor and Me) are equal in essence but different in function. We have the same powerful capabilities but just operate differently.

"I will not leave you helpless because my additional gift to you is my Book. In the Book, I present a series of promises, commandments, instructions and words of wisdom, encouragement, celebrations and disciplinary actions. Make sure you read it, study it and apply its principles to your life; because at various points on your journey, you will need to rely heavily upon it."

Human trusted The Gift-Source and was excited because The Gift-Source's word never failed. Plus, The Gift-Source knows what is best for everyone.

Having returned home, Human anxiously waited for the gifts to arrive. As promised, the first gift came but it was not what Human expected.

"Who are you?," Human asked the unexpected gift.

"Hello, my name is Chaos," replied the gift.

Totally shocked, Human returned to The Gift-Source and asked for the meaning of such an unexpected gift. Human also asked The Gift-Source to take back the unwanted gift.

In response, The Gift-Source allowed the gift to remain and then speak for itself.

Chapter 1

MEET CHAOS

$\mathcal{M}$eet Chaos.

"Let me introduce myself," said Chaos. "You may know me by my other names like Pandemonium, Mayhem, Bedlam, Anarchy or Mass Chaos (my nickname for Total Chaos). I use those aliases as needed, depending on the situation. I am located in every assignment and challenge.

"I may operate through darkness but The Gift-Source ultimately brings Light to the situations in which I'm located.

"Here's how my family and I operate. I have several children but Fear and Panic are the most infamous. They are the advanced team. When they work in cooperation, Confusion shows up and begins its work.

"My family members are avid painters. We paint with dark and bleak shades of color. So when you look at one of our pictures, things look bleak and hopeless. But what many don't realize is that it's all a façade. That's right. Our pictures give the appearance of things not working out for a gift-recipient's best interest. So, a lot of people give into despair and become discouraged. Most times, they totally give up, believing that things will never change.

"I hear your unasked questions. You are wondering: Where is my place of origin? What is the cause of me? Where did I come from?"

Seeing that it had Human's total attention, Chaos continued with the introduction.

"I was conceived through my originator's rebellion and insubordination to The Gift-Source. My originator is also known as the enemy.

"I am most notorious in crises and storms because that is where Fear and Panic really show their skill set. They make me so proud when they work together. I thrive with my assistants, total Disorder and Confusion. I cannot function without them especially in crises like epidemics, divisive moments, pandemics, wars, recessions, plagues, civil unrest, depressions and other scary times.

"I'm versatile because I can operate anywhere in anyone's life... at work... at home... in relationships... in government... in schools... in any sacred institution... You name it and you can find me anywhere and somewhere. I'm everywhere but my operations can only go so far, especially if The Gift-Source is present.

"I have several disguises like medical chaos, family chaos, political chaos, financial chaos, salvational chaos, and others. I'm sure you've seen some of them in your life."

Chaos continued, "As you can see, my span is wide and my influence is vast. My résumé is extensive. I'm unexpected but sometimes, necessary."

"I don't understand," Human said in bewilderment. "This still does not explain how you are a gift."

"I have a job to do and I show up in various ways," Chaos bragged. "On certain levels, people walk with me daily. I can come by way of unresolved grief, guilt or emotional pain — usually more than people can bear. On the other hand, I can come through disappointment in family, friends, career or circumstances in general. I can even come when life seems to be going well."

Needless to say, Human was confused and panicked saying, "This can't be right! There must be a mistake! Gifts are supposed to be enjoyable. How can I enjoy you if you thrive on disorder and confusion? You are not what I expected! I trusted The Gift-Source! I thought The Gift-Source knew what was best for me! I thought The Gift-Source operated in my best interest! What makes you a gift?"

"My giftedness applies in many ways. For example, The Gift-Source uses me to shift paradigms. I'm here to help you move to the next level of living. I can help you discover your true purpose. Through me, The Gift-Source can send Insight to give you new ideas... or help you solve that problem... or help you get organized... or make that critical decision... or fix that relationship... or reach that child... or pass that test... or achieve that dream... or _____ (You fill in the blank). You get the picture, right? Out of me, comes order; and you get blessed in the process.

"So, calm down. Be anxious for nothing. In every situation by prayer and petition with gratefulness, present your requests to The Gift-Source. When you do, you will experience a peace that is indescribable; and your heart and mind will be guarded by The Son.

"Your request for a gift has truly been granted. You just did not expect me — Chaos. I am a gift that came wrapped in an unexpected package.

"I'm also a good educator. I have some things to teach you. Let's begin. First, I'll teach you how valuable I can be."

> # Your request for a gift has truly been granted. You just did not expect me — Chaos.

Chapter 2

THE VALUE OF CHAOS

"That's right. I actually have some value," Chaos said with a pompous tone, arms folded and nose in the air.

"For example, I'm used to shift paradigms. Think about it. Some of the greatest inventions were created after people encountered me. Some of the most successful businesses were birthed because I shifted paradigms. And some of the best advancements, medications and signature government legislation came about because I showed up.

"Remember the bubonic plague? What about the Irish potato famine? How about the Great Depression? Remember the Civil Rights Movement? What about the great recession? Yes, those were chaotic moments in history but some good came out of each one of them.

"Think about it. You have antibiotics to treat the bubonic plague today. Scientists discovered what was killing the potatoes and found the cure that eventually led to the end of the famine. The Great Depression led to the government's creation of the Federal Deposit Insurance Corporation. You know it as the FDIC that protects your bank deposits. The American civil rights movement led to the passing of federal legislation outlawing racial discrimination. And the government intervened in the great recession to prevent an economic depression.

"Let's make it personal. What about those chaotic moments in your life? You've had some. Or you may be having some right now. This too shall pass. It's sad for me, Chaos, that it will end; but that's great news for you because trouble don't last always.

"I know it's painful. It's difficult. It's hard to forgive the human who caused you so much pain. I know you want to give up but you will get through it.

"Weeping may endure for a night, but joy will come in the morning. It may not be tomorrow morning but the joy will come. And someday, you will understand why you went through the difficulties. I promise you that some good will result from your chaotic situations, no matter how horrible they are. I know it's difficult to see that right now but hold on; a change will come. You are going to make it through the chaos.

"Every individual on earth was created for a specific purpose. However, it's unfortunate that many never realize or live out their purpose because they don't know who they are or why they exist.

"Look at yourself. You have a purpose in life and I can help you discover it. If you are living beneath your potential, I go into action. If you are operating in an unauthorized area, I go into action. If you decide to operate outside of your purpose, I go into action.

"If you decide to stay in your comfort zone, I could show up to either help you move to the next level or make your life miserable. It depends on how you receive me. Matter of fact, I do some of my best work in comfort zones.

"The Gift-Source creates order out of me. The Gift-Source's spoken word is to create order out of your chaotic life. Remember, you were designed for a certain purpose. You were created to be a solution to a problem. However, when you fail to become that spoken purpose, I show up.

I can initiate circumstances to bring you in or take you to where you're supposed to be.

"You see, many are engaged in survival living and not abundant living. One of the goals of The Gift-Source is to not just give you life but give you an abundant life.

"I have an automatic seat at the table in disorderly environments. I'm present if you are living in opposition to The Gift-Source's will or purpose for your life. And, if you operate outside of The Gift-Source's purposed will, you are in a place where you're not supposed to be.

"I know of many who were chosen to carry out a specific purpose in life but chose to live outside their created purpose. What was the result? Me! Chaos!

"The tragedy does not end there. If you operate outside of your true purpose, you put those around you in jeopardy too, especially when you are in or are headed to a place you're not supposed to be.

"There is value in me, Chaos; because I can initiate circumstances to bring you in or take you to where you're supposed to be. So I sometimes serve as the force to get you on target and back on track with your true purpose. Many will not grow or benefit because they only see me and not the gift I am or can be.

"Let's talk about your destination. The Gift-Source's purposed will for your life is empowered through The Gift-Source's spoken word. The means, ability, privilege, and capacity to reach your potential is a journey with a destination. For example, one time, The Gift-Source's Son told some gift-recipients to get in a boat and said, 'Let us cross over to the other side of a sea.'

"During the journey, a terrible storm arose. In that storm, waves broke over the boat, so that it was nearly swamped. I was present that day too. In fact, I was in the midst of it all. The Son was at the back of the boat, sleeping on a cushion.

"Unable to handle the storm themselves, the gift-recipients woke up The Son and asked, 'Don't you care if we drown?'

"The Son got up and told the storm, "Peace be still." Then the wind died down and so did I. I had to calm down. I had no choice.

"The Son asked the gift-recipients, "Why are you so afraid? Do you still not trust Me?

"That boat episode presents an answer to the probing question about The Gift-Source's purposed will for your life and the faith encountered with destination in mind.

"It seems that when your relationships are strongest, I invade your space. Your purposed will is not in your being but in your becoming. It's not in where you are, but where you must move to and it is always toward your destination on the 'other side.'

"That brings me to my next point. I can move you toward your created purpose. Since The Gift-Source knows how you are uniquely designed and created, The Gift-Source will always be present with you if you allow that presence into your life.

"The Gift-Source's presence will bring peace and order to your personal experience with me, Chaos. Peace and order may not show up right away, but they will eventually come.

"Look again at the boat episode I just told you about. The Son was on the boat with some gift-recipients and a storm arose. Buffeted by the winds and waves, the crew was about to lose their lives and their hope.

"There is another situation in which a similar storm occurred. I , Chaos, know about it because I was there wreaking havoc too. This particular storm arose because one gift-recipient was out of order and out of place. In fact, the gift-recipient chose not to operate within The Gift-Source's purposed will. In this case, a storm showed up because persons on the ship were where they were supposed to be, except the gift recipient who had fallen asleep.

"That sleeper was the reason for the storm and my presence. The sleeper was the answer to the storm. When the sleeper confessed to the ship's crew the reason for the storm, the crew threw the sleeper overboard. Then, the thunder lost its voice. The movement of lightening was paralyzed. The water and waves found a place to retire. And order was brought to me, Chaos. By the way, the sleeper survived in spite of being thrown overboard. Remember that The Gift-Source is ultimately in charge and took care of the sleeper in spite of its wrongdoing.

"Consider this: What if you and The Gift-Source were on a ship together and encountered a major storm but The Gift-Source was asleep? What would you do?"

Chapter 3

GETTING THROUGH CHAOS

"When you recognize The Gift-Source's presence through a quality relationship and learn your faith-lessons through the storms or through me, Chaos, The Gift-Source will then take you to the place where you're supposed to be —'to the other side' — and reveal your purpose.

"On the other side, there is a need. On the other side, there is someone whom people gave up on and threw up their hands in frustration. On the other side, there is your purpose waiting to be fulfilled. Others may count you out, but The Gift-Source has time for you.

"Yes, there are plenty of examples of my work because The Gift Source uses me in various ways through my disguises like relationship, salvational, and medical chaos.

"For instance, there once was a gift-recipient located at a well one day but was in relationship-chaos. The Gift-Source through The Son, was present and gave the gift of salvation-deliverance.

"There was another gift-recipient who climbed a tree because the recipient was plagued with salvational chaos. The Gift-Source, through The Son, showed up and said, 'Come down from the tree.' That gift-recipient was known for being a swindler and thief; but after meeting The Son, the gift-recipient renounced wicked ways and promised to financially repay those who had been robbed.

"Another recipient experienced medical chaos and 12 years of suffering as a result. Then, The Gift-Source (through The Son) showed up and gave the gift of healing.

"You see, in all these experiences with me, Chaos, The Gift-Source speaks a word and brings order and peace. The Gift-Source designed you with purpose and on purpose. Through a faith-based relationship, The Gift-Source will speak a word and bring order to your purpose and peace to your life.

"The Son assures you, that The Guidance-Counselor, Whom The Gift-Source will send, will teach you all things and will remind you of everything that has been said to you. The Son leaves peace with you. The Son gives you His peace but not like the world gives. Even in the chaos, do not let your hearts be troubled and do not be afraid.

"I, Chaos, told you that I'm unexpected, but sometimes necessary. If it weren't for me, you wouldn't leave your comfort zone.

"I may be out of control at times but Gift Giver knows how to keep me under control, bring order out of me and bring good out of me.

"To maximize your potential and to live the abundant life, healing must occur. The healing of relationships within your family or community must take place. Trust must be established. Goals must be set. Plans must be developed and implemented.

"I could go on and on but I must remind you of something. Don't be discouraged because I am in your life, because the Guidance-Counselor is alive and well. The Gift-Source is getting ready to speak a Word to your situation and that Word is: 'Let there be...' Sounds strange, doesn't it? Let me explain further.

"In the beginning of time, The Gift-Source uttered a series of 'Let There Be's' and I, Chaos, changed into order. The simple suggestion here is catch hold to the spiritual waves that are riding *through* me; because that is where The Gift-Source is. The Gift-Source is not in me but is operating through me and bringing order out of me.

"Here's how it's done: I'm used to deliver you and then develop you. So many are discouraged and frustrated. They are giving up because they're experiencing me through one or more of my other disguises — social, mental, physical or spiritual chaos.

"However, much of your mental chaos is self-inflicted because you develop comfort zones in the old things, better known as **tradition**.

"Many have a desire for change but ironically resist change. I show up because remember, you do not exist in a state of being but in a state of *becoming*. f you desire a new level of living... if you are going to live the abundant life... if you want to live your real purpose...you must increase the quality of your faith.

"The Gift-Source is getting ready to do a new thing in your life. **The core problem is you don't really mind the changes but you really don't want to change.** You need to change some things into better things. Work with what you have in order to make it into what it ought to be. Do you see how you can actually move me, Chaos, from my present state to creation?

THE CONVERSION OF Y2K

"Let's go back a few decades. Remember Y2K — the year 2000? Back in 1999, I threatened to disrupt all areas of life. At that time, computers and networks were vital and still are in things like communication, travel, finances, food supply, water supply and safety. Thanks to The Gift-Source enabling scientists, computer operators and other experts, my potential threat to unleash my secret weapon and alter ego Mass Chaos was circumvented.

"Back then, computer specialists were concerned that about computers crashing and if the systems continued to run, then the data and calculations would be produced in error. Consequently, if one system fed into a larger system of networks, the results would be catastrophic with miscalculations on a national and international level. Lives would simply crash. They would not be able to move forward with dysfunctional or untrustworthy relationships serving as the foundation. In a word, there was the possibility that the entire world, beginning in the year 2000, would be operating on a dysfunctional system.

"Human, you may be wondering what does Y2K have to do with you? Think about it like this: I become order through growth. Out of me, you can meet your challenges by eliminating the historical models of reacting and fear. You can be proactive and courageous instead.

"The consequences of failing to respond properly to me , Chaos, is a matter of importance. If I'm not addressed properly, you will not be able to function properly. It's like trying to put a square peg into a round hole. If there is a serious malfunction, there is a possibility to fix it after the occurrence. You can survive. You still have hope. "Do an assessment of your life. You must answer and deal with the following issues: Where are you now in life? Where do you want to go? What are your immediate, short range and long range goals? How will your plans be developed, implemented, and evaluated?

"The Gift-Source has a broader view for your life and is doing a new thing. Will you not grow or benefit because you only see me, Chaos, and not The Gift-Source operating in your situation? The things that you are fighting or trying to avoid, you need to be shaping with the teachings of The Gift-Source."

"If the Y2K problem had not been corrected, computers around the world would have crashed. Likewise, the consequences of not responding to The Gift-Source will have devastating effects on your life both now and in the future.

"Imagine this consequence facing a reality of hopelessness, no chance of joy, or no peace. I want to encourage you to think about and pray about the consequences. This is not a time to sit idle. It is not a time to be quiet. It is a time of evaluation, a time of preparing, a time to extend The Gift-Source's wisdom. Remember, even in my existence, The Gift-Source is doing a new thing with you. You may not understand what is happening right now but later you will. So, walk by faith, not by sight."

DOS: DYSFUNCTIONAL OPERATING SYSTEMS

"Here's something else about me, Chaos, to consider. I enjoy operating in dysfunctional systems. Some systems are dysfunctional because they are outdated. Can you imagine trying to travel today from South Carolina to California by using a wagon with horses? No, of course you can't. The paradigm shifted many years ago as society went from using wagons to bicycles to driving cars and flying airplanes.

"I told you before that The Gift Source creates order out of me. Furthermore, The Gift-Source refuses to operate or function without there being order. Keep in mind that I have no shape or substance. The Gift-Source refuses to operate, function or participate in my realm.

> **...out of the chaos, in spite of the uncertainty, The Gift-Source is fine-tuning your purpose and moving you toward your destiny**

"Your life changes as a result of non-growth on the one hand and growth on the other hand. Change brings with it pain presented in defining moments of frustration, anger, depression and sometimes discontentment. If the movement is not seamless, change brings on Chaos. That's me!

"Understand that everybody wants to see change but no one wants to change. However, out of the chaos, in spite of the uncertainty, The Gift-Source is fine-tuning your purpose and moving you toward your destiny. As you move from season to season, from relationship and from location to purpose-destination, if you walk by faith, you can arrest your fears because when The Gift-Source gives an 'ordered movement,' the way has already been made.

"And how The Gift-Source meets the needs of gift-recipients depend upon the season they are in. There are times when The Gift-Source leads and other times, when The Gift-Source protects. There are other times when The Gift-Source is simultaneously light and darkness — meaning, The Gift-Source is Light to the gift-recipients and darkness to those who try to derail the recipients.

"Faith is the key in the life of every gift-recipient. Now what that means is if faith is key to your response to The Gift-Source's shifting seasons, it does not matter how good you become at being a gift-recipient. It does not matter how much you got your 'stuff together.' If you don't keep your faith growing and moving, you will lack trust in The Gift-Source because the Book is clear and on point. The Book says, without faith, it is impossible to please The Gift-Source. If you don't trust The Gift-Source, then you will have a hard time getting through me, Chaos."

Chapter 4

WHAT MAKES CHAOS, CHAOS?

Chaos noticed Human's questioning expression and continued, "You want to know another reason why I might show up? It's because The Gift-Source is improving or creating something new and good around your painful condition.

"So, maybe you need to make a decision to not get mixed up, caught up or involved with me because The Gift-Source does not endorse my activities. If you want to have a fruitful, fulfilling life, you should not want to be in anything in which The Gift-Source is not going to participate.

"Make this the season you stay away from me and my kinfolk. Also, stay away from others who have no substance and make no sense. Stay away from my situations, my conditions and my relationships.

"Matter of fact you ought to declare your life as a 'no chaos zone.' And be sure to tell others that you are a 'no chaos zone.' Tell them not to come to you with foolishness. Don't try to be their friend if they are not going anywhere in life. Don't let them be all up in your business if they are not operating on sincere purpose. Why would you want somebody in your life who has no substance and whose actions make no sense anyway? Remember, you are a 'no chaos zone.'

"And you can tell me too, 'Since I declare a 'no chaos zone,' I don't want you, Chaos, in my house, friendships, partnerships or fellowships.' And it's okay to tell me that. I can handle it because I have plenty of other opportunities to keep me busy."

Before Human could respond, Chaos continued teaching the lesson.

"Make sure your decisions meet The Gift-Source's approval. If The Gift-Source does not approve your decisions, then your life will be chaotic. Now here is the good news revealed in creation. The Gift-Source has the power to step into me, Chaos, and turn me into cosmos. I exist when there is no shape, no sense and no substance.

"Cosmos is when there is shape and a sense of order — meaning, there is purpose and substance. The Gift-Source's got a way of stepping into mess that makes no sense, speaking a word over the mess and turning the mess into a miracle. The Gift-Source did not just do that to the chaos around you. The Gift-Source did that to the chaos that was in you too.

"Many gift-recipients are and were a mess with no shape — making no sense; but The Gift-Source stepped in and brought order to their chaotic lives.

"The Gift-Source can step into your chaotic situation and take all its pieces and shape it into something beautiful. By the time The Gift-Source is finished working in the situation, the pieces will have meaning and substance.

"If your life today is in disarray, give your life and problems to The Gift-Source now. The Gift-Source's got the power to turn them into something wonderful. You do not need a new life per se. You just need The Gift-Source in your life now.

"If you try to fix your life on your own, then more than likely you will produce me, Chaos. Yet, now is the time to move out of my territory and watch The Gift-Source do what only The Gift-Source can do. The Gift-Source is able to do exceedingly, abundantly above all that you can ask, think or imagine.

"The Gift-Source's nature is one of order. A second principle that is apparent in The Gift-Source's work is the necessity for connection for purposeful living. When The Gift-Source creates, things are connected and everything relates to one another.

"For example, The Gift-Source made water relate to fish... water relate to grass... grass relate to cows... The Gift-Source did not just let grass relate to grass and

> ## The Gift-Source can step into your chaotic situation and take all its pieces and shape it into something beautiful.

water relate to water or fish relate to fish. For all of them to work purposefully, they had to be connected to something diverse.

"The power of connection is in the power of diversity. Real power comes when everyone or everything does not look alike or act alike. Real power comes through different backgrounds, different gifts and talents.

"If every gift-recipient would take all their diverse gifts and talents, remove egos and walk into what The Gift-Source has purposed them to do, they would have better communities. No matter the age, stage, race, creed or color, their past or present status – anyone can participate in the diversity.

"When recipients work out their diversity, The Gift-Source will create an effective transforming group of persons that eyes have not seen nor ears have heard.

"The Gift-Source does everything with connectivity and purpose and does not measure importance the way you do.

"You want proof? Here we go. Once upon a time, The Gift-Source created two great lights. One was a greater light to rule the day. That light is otherwise known as the sun. And the other was a lesser light to rule the night. The lesser light is the moon.

"Greater and lesser suggests importance right? Wrong! You and your fellow gift-recipients or humans often measure importance by titles, money, education degrees or longevity. The Gift-Source does not measure importance and value like you all do.

"Look at one gift-recipient's ordeal with a tempter and the temptation of comparison. One day, that gift-recipient compared self with The Gift-Source who has all knowledge. Comparing self to The Gift-Source is senseless.

"But the gift-recipient gave into temptation anyway because by comparison, the gift-recipient did not measure up to The Gift-Source.

"So the tempter (who by the way, is also my originator) said, 'By comparison, The Gift-Source knows if you give into the temptation, you will be just as smart as The Gift-Source.'

"So the gift-recipient began comparing its own knowledge to The Gift-Source's knowledge. The gift-recipient said, 'I don't compare; so if I want to be equal, I got to give into the temptation.'

"The temptation of comparison is alive and well today because jealousy and haters are alive and well. The only reason those two things raise their ugly head is because you get caught up in the temptation of comparison. Then, when you mix comparison with your own insecurity and you compare yourself to others, you feel like you don't measure up.

"Moreover, you feel like you got to tear down others in order to feel important; or you do all you can to try to come up to their level because you are caught up in comparing self to others. Why? Because society deems how importance and value are supposed to be measured.

"Here is what the gift-recipient who gave into the temptation of comparison missed. The gift-recipient could not compare because the recipient was a gift-recipient, not The Gift-Source. In other words, The Gift-Source and the gift-recipient were totally different in nature with totally different functions.

"And since the gift-recipient did not have the functional responsibility that The Gift-Source had, the recipient would not need to have the knowledge The Gift-Source had.

"Why are you around here comparing yourself to somebody else when you are not them and they are not you? Not having what they have does not make you less of a human. Your importance does not come from what you have or what you are called or how well-known you are. Importance comes from functioning in your purpose.

"I said earlier that the sun is deemed as the greater light and the moon is the lesser light. Most would be offended by the designation 'lesser.'

"Be careful in measuring your value and importance. If you were the moon, you would probably be upset with The Gift-Source terming you as lesser. You would say, 'How dare you call me the lesser!" because to you, lesser does not sound as important or not as valuable. To you, it probably means inferior or subordinate.

"What you fail to see is that one of the lights was called 'lesser' because of its size not because of its importance. But remember, The Gift-Source made two great lights.

"If you take your eyes off the term 'lesser,' you will see the first description which said that both lights were great. Yes. They were different in size but they were the same in greatness because they both functioned where The Gift-Source purposed them to function.

"So, if you feel like or have been made to feel that you are less than or are not as important because you have less money...or because you have less education... or because you are single... or because you have a cubicle and not an office... or because you drive a car that is 20 years old... or because you are living in your grandmother's house instead of your own... count it all joy!

"I know you cannot celebrate that because others seem to have it all together, but you choose to live in a garment of dysfunction-insecurity. As a result, you tend to define yourself as being lesser than everybody else.

"But here is the point: You may have lesser but you can be just as great if you stick to who you are and what The Gift-Source has purposed you to do.

"You are just as great as anybody else. No, you don't have what they have. Your money is funny. You made some mistakes in life. You made some bad decisions but you have been gifted by The Gift-Source. Therefore, you are just as great as anybody else.

"Be you. Do you and The Gift-Source will take care of the rest. Just be who The Gift-Source made you to be and you are already great.

"Say to yourself, 'I am great. The reason I am great is because I have a great Gift-Source who invested greatly in me.'"

Chapter 5

CHANGING THE TIDES OF CHAOS

"Consider the moon again. The moon can teach you some things about how you ought to function. One thing about the moon is that it casts light on the earth when the sun is absent. Let me strangely suggest to you that this is one of *your* jobs.

"As a gift-recipient, one of your jobs is to cast light on situations. The Gift-Source is *the* Light and gives you power to be light in dark situations. What does it mean to be the light? Answer: When you show up in a location, darkness ought to go away."

"Remember darkness is associated with me, Chaos; which means your presence ought to bring an end to my existence. As a gift-recipient, you cannot go into darkness acting like darkness.

"If you are really light, then when you show up, all the ongoing darkness has got to flee. Consider this. When you show up, that is why some gift-recipients on your job don't like you because when you walk into the room, they get uncomfortable. They start gossiping, lying and cussing; and they just wish you would leave. You cannot afford to leave because a part of your job description is to deal with darkness.

"You cannot go into the darkness as a light participating in the ongoing darkness. When you show up, darkness has got to go. When you come in with light, others should not feel comfortable around you gossiping. When they are around you, they ought not be comfortable lying, starting rumors and destroying other people's character.

"Go back to the beginning... You will see what The Gift-Source, who is *the* Light, did. Light showed up.

"When Light showed up, it revealed how messy things were. The Light revealed shoreless seas, tossing waters and land without substance above the sea.

"So even today, the Light exposes everything that needs to be fixed. When you show up, you ought to show up with a right character and with The Guidance-Counselor's special power called the anointing. Ask The Gift-Source for a praying spirit and prayer power. Let your light so shine."

"I must declare that if you are going to be light, you got to start stepping into the darkness and telling the darkness, 'You cannot stay here.'

"Don't miss this," warned Chaos. "Light exposes things that need to be fixed. If you are not making a situation better and if you are not exposing situations that need to be fixed, then you are not functioning properly in your light-assignment or in your anointing.

"I know what you're thinking. You're saying to yourself, 'That's what I'm doing. I'm fixing it.' Wrong answer again! Fixing does not mean fixing it your way.

"You don't fix it your way. In the beginning, when the Light revealed what was messed up, The Gift-Source was the One Who fixed it. Don't try to assume The Gift-Source's role. Instead, step out of the way. Let your light shine and expose, then give the mess to The Gift-Source. Let The Gift-Source do what's best and that is fixing the problem and therefore, bringing order to the chaos.

"The only way the moon can shine is by reflecting the sun which means you will not shine just because you are called the moon. Your moon-title does not make you shine. You got to position yourself to be in the track of the sun so its light can bounce off you and give a reflection.

"Moon brightness and moon size is very small as related to the brightness of the sun. The sun is 400 times greater than the moon. In other words, without the sun, there is nothing to the moon.

"Likewise, without The Gift-Source, you would be nothing. Without The Gift-Source, you would surely fail. Without The Gift-Source, you would be drifting like a ship without a sail.

"Your main responsibility is to reflect light in the absence of the sun. You are the light of the world. You cannot be hidden. When light goes into darkness, the darkness goes away."

FAKING FULLNESS

'The moon does not shine the same every day and it does not fake its fullness. The moon can change from full to a quarter, to a crescent to darkness. The moon is not always lit up at full capacity. There are some days where the moon is more visible. On some days, you see its light and darkness but there are days when it does not shine as bright. Look at yourself. There are some days that you do not shine as bright as you do on other days.

"There are some days when you are full and bright. On those days, The Gift-Source's spirit is in you and you're on full. You are loving your enemies and loving people even the ones who are using you.

"But then, there are some days when you are half-full. If people catch the wrong side of you, then they catch your dark side and they may not see your 'lovingness.' Yes, you still have some dark areas that you struggle with.

"Be real with yourself. You got some areas in your life that have not reached the light yet. You got some weaknesses. You got some short comings. You got some areas under construction. You got some areas that you need help with.

"Be honest with yourself and admit that there are areas you thought were healed but they were only in remission. You did not know it until you saw that other human again or you experienced that same event again.

"Now back to the moon. The moon's dark sides come out on the sides that are not close to the Sun. You see, when you got areas in your life that you are trying to hold onto...when you got areas you do not want to deal with, they will remain dark. That is why you have to be honest and real enough to admit where you are weak, who makes you weak and what makes you weak so you can give the weakness to The Gift-Source to handle.

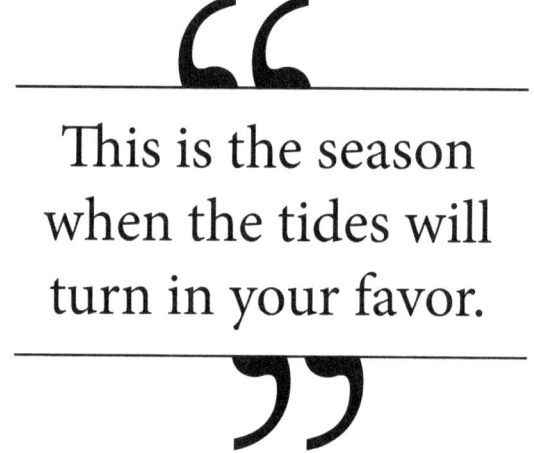

This is the season when the tides will turn in your favor.

"You are walking around talking about 'I can handle things by myself.'

"One of the problems some gift-recipients have is they fake being full. They have this 'I-don't-ever-mess-up' attitude or an 'I- don't-ever-have-a-problem' mentality.

"They walk around with their nose stuck up in the air as if they are better than everybody else. The real reason they do not do what they really want to do is because age or health will not let them.

"So again, sometimes you are on full and sometimes you are on half. And sometimes you get eclipses. Scientifically speaking, an eclipse happens when the earth comes between the moon and the sun.

"You see, when you let something come between you and The Gift-Source, especially The Son... you are living in an eclipsed state. Word of advice: Don't be eclipsed.

"Don't let nothing or nobody come between you and The Son. Don't let it ruin your relationship with The Gift-Source.

"Make a decision and say, 'I don't care what comes into my life. I don't care how much trouble gets in my way. I will not be eclipsed.'

"Need more convincing? Ok, be persuaded that neither death nor life nor angels or principalities nor things present or things to come shall be able to separate you from The Gift-Source's love for you. You may have days when you are full or when you are half-full but let nothing eclipse you.

"Some would have you to believe that you must be perfect. No one is perfect but you can be better. Maintain your relationship with The Gift-Source. Come on now. It is about progress.

"But be warned. Occasional turbulence can hit the atmosphere. Whether the moon is full or half, whether it is a crescent or whether it is an eclipse or not, it is still the moon. Likewise, you are still a gift-recipient.

"Look at it like this. When you make horrible mistakes, you still belong to your parents, don't you? Now look at The Gift-Source. Even on your dark days, because you are still a gift-recipient, if you admit and acknowledge your wrongdoing, The Gift-Source is faithful and just to forgive you.

"Say to yourself, 'I made a mistake but I am still The Gift-Source's recipient. I made bad decisions but I am still The Gift-Source's recipient. When I fall short and fall down, I am still The Gift-Source's recipient.'"

POWER TO CHANGE THE TIDES

"The moon has power to change the tides. Every day, the moon pulls the waters of the ocean up along the shore into the mouths of rivers. As large as the ocean is (as powerful as the sea is), it has no power against the pull of the moon.

"Let's put that in the context of your personal situation. You tend to believe that some of the storms you are in are stronger than you; but you must know that no matter how rough the seas get, you got the power within you to change the tides. So when you start speaking, even the storms have to behave.

"As powerful as storms are by causing torrential winds, tornados, hurricanes and more, storms have no power to resist the influence of the moon.

"Likewise, if The Son is with you, you got the power over every personal storm. You got the power to be still in the storm. You got the power to be at peace in the storm. You got the power to walk in the storm.

"You got the power to influence the tides. Just like the moon pulls, you got the power to pull down some stuff and pull up some stuff. This is the season when the tides will turn in your favor.

"So yes, it has been rough. It has been tough with personal problems... medical problems... work problems... family problems... school problems... financial problems. The spouse and children are acting up. Things did not happen like you wanted them to but this is the season where the tides will turn.

"Your season is here. You are in charge of the tides of your life. You can make the tides in your life turn. You have the power because of the authority of your faith. You can speak things that are not as though they were. You have the power to change the tides.

"Your power is in your tongue — that which you speak and what you say to yourself. Life and death are in the power of your tongue. That is why you must be careful what you say. If you speak negativity, then you will have negativity. On the flip side, if you speak positivity, you will have positivity.

"Remember what I am telling you. The tides are turning in your life. Like the moon, you are changing the tides in your life.

"How do you change the tides? You begin the process by acknowledging the power of The Gift-Source. You must walk by faith and not by sight.

"When you learn to reverence The Gift-Source only, you turn the tides. When you commit to change in your life, you turn the tides.

"I know you are ready for the tides to turn. You are tired of crying... tired of sleepless nights... tired of trying to make ends meet... This is your season. The tides will turn.

"Now, you don't have to wait until the tides come in. You can celebrate and rejoice right now because The Gift-Source has made you some promises.

"You don't see it yet but it is coming. Your miracle is coming. Your breakthrough is coming. Your blessing is coming. Your favor is coming.

"Be thankful. Declare for your life including your home... your work... your dreams... your vision... a 'chaos-free' zone.

"If you were to take a vote right now, those in favor of making your life a 'chaos-free' zone by reflecting the power of The Son, say 'I.'

"Opposers say, 'Nay.' There are no opposers. Therefore, the 'I's' have it.

"Now go and do what needs to be done to turn the tides for the betterment of your life. Then watch me , Chaos, transform and become order instead of Chaos.

Chapter 6

FROM CHAOS TO ORDER

"So, that's most of my story. I can lead to the destruction of your own self, families, communities and ultimately the world; but through me, The Gift-Source can still provide revelation. If you undergird that revelation with discipline, you can have ordered purpose for your life.

"As I conclude my teaching lesson, you must examine the present condition of your life – what its role and impact will and must be. Through the empowerment of The Guidance Counselor, the Book will equip you - make fit, prepare, train – to help you discover what you are called to do.

"In one of the Book chapters, The Gift-Source advises you on how to prepare for the enemy's coming. You must allow The Gift-Source to outfit you with some full armor. When you put on the full armor, you will be equipped to take your stand against the enemy's schemes and attacks.

"So often I hear gift-recipients in their conversation repeat time and time again, 'I was put on earth for a reason.' Every individual was created on purpose and with purpose. Every individual was created to be a solution to a problem.

"Your purpose is divinely endowed and external forces cannot shift or change your purpose without The Gift-Source's authorization. So many gift-recipients with great potential live defeated lives because they allow my originator (the enemy) to distract them through skillful deception.

"I'm not trying to be clever but clear. To live a life on purpose, reinforced with an evolving vision, there must be counsel and revelation from The Gift-Source or from one of the special agents sent by The Gift-Source.

"Every special agent may be called but not sent with the revelation for *your* particular purpose. Sometimes you and other gift-recipients seek personal purpose and destiny. In the process of seeking, I'm created simply because so many well-intentioned gift-recipients are listening to the wrong agents.

"The chaos in your life is not necessarily punishment but an invitation to go by faith to the next growth level for your signature assignment (ordered purpose). Here's the formula:

CHAOS + <u>REVELATION</u> = ORDERED PURPOSE
DISCIPLINE

"A signature assignment is also a call to preparation and you don't want to be unprepared in a prepared place.

"Come with me to explore the final leg of the journey to move from chaos to order.

"Look at 3 C's:
Number one, chaos in the family.
Number two, conflict vs. gift.
Number three, contact with The Son."

CHAOS IN THE FAMILY

"Listen to me carefully," said Chaos. "The house is on fire. The baby is burning up and you are over in a corner picking up pins. Do you want to get rid of me? Then stop minoring on major things and stop majoring on minor things.

"An assessment of those who are in contentious struggles gives you a good indication as to why my originator seems to have such a strategic advantage.

"You have too many gift-recipients busy taking revenge for wounds sustained in unauthorized relationships. Additionally, they are functioning in non-delegated areas of authority that they are of little use in some cases and are of no use in other cases. Consequently, they become instruments for their own destruction.

What some gift-recipients do not realize is that their behavior is the primary cause for the visible chaos.

"Many are pre-occupied with self. Therefore, communities are left without meaningful impact by its community institutions. And what's the result? That's right; me , Chaos! Your schools and marketplace have become targets for wickedness. As a result, the world is left without any significant influence of faith. The result is me, Chaos, in the... home, church, community, state, nation and the world.

"My originator's rebellious, insubordinate spirit lives on in humans operating in areas of authority without being under authority. What some gift recipients do not realize is that their behavior is the primary cause for the visible chaos. The spirit within is released into the atmosphere and that seed, that spirit begets after its own kind.

"You don't believe me? Think about it this way: In the military, there is leadership with authorized, delegated authority. Everyone under that leadership is expected to follow leadership and leadership orders. If everyone is operating where they are supposed to be, then there is order, not chaos.

"If your spirit will not allow you to be under The Gift-Source's authority, then you pass on that same spirit to your own house and in some cases, the family unit. Your family will not accept your authority in *your* house because you've simply manifested and passed on a spirit of rebellion and defiance.

"Look at another example. When you reproduce and have offspring who are repeatedly nurtured by television shows (including cartoons) with perpetual violence, movies that glorify violence, music with explicit lyrics and violence, videos with violence, computer games with violence, the Internet with violence, social media celebrating violence and the like, then you are creating an appetite for violence. So is there any wonder society experiences things like massacres at schools, concerts, shopping malls, churches and other public gatherings.

"Why? Because most likely, the spirit that children inherited from their parents coupled with the spirits they acquire from their environment and other means, eventually express themselves in the physical realm. Chaos is the bottom line!

"Now, this may not happen in some cases. But the groundwork has been laid for me to operate freely.

"Many years ago, The Gift-Source was invited to participate in public places like schools and other gatherings. His commandments could even be posted in public facilities. The Gift-Source was an important factor in the home and society in general; but my originator came in and began to plant ideas of independence and self-importance. So humans assumed they could handle things themselves and began to invoke arguments like separation of church and state.

"Subsequently, many grew to believe that The Gift-Source's authority interfered with their pursuits; and there was no need for The Gift-Source's help anymore. Eventually, The Gift-Source's name was barely mentioned — if at all — in their own homes. I applauded the people for adopting that attitude because it created the perfect environment for me and my relatives to operate unobstructed.

"Remember, The Gift-Source will not, and neither will The Son operate in areas where they are not invited. So gradually, their presence was no longer welcome in most places. For me, that meant I was free to run rampant and assume many aliases.

"Now at first, it was subtle. No one noticed the changing tides for the worse; but today, society reaps the consequences of their **EGO** – Easing **The Gift-Source** Out of the picture.

"As you look back and observe what's happening now, it is safe to say that if The Gift-Source is in the midst, gift-recipients are covered. They are protected. He stands between me, Chaos, and them. If The Gift-Source is present, then I'm hindered. I cannot operate as freely as I would like. Or sometimes, through The Gift-Source's permissive will, I operate with limitations.

At this point, Human immediately objected and raised a question. "No, what you're saying can't be right! What about the situations where The Gift-Source's recipients died and were killed anyway? Several cases in point, "What about slavery... the Holocaust... the Civil Rights marches... 911 (September 11, 2011)... the 2020 Pandemic...? There were also massacres in some of The Gift-Source's houses of worship. In all those instances and others, it looks like you and your cohorts were free to steal, kill and destroy."

With grief and skepticism, Human continued. "Your argument does not mesh with the fact that some of The Gift-Source's recipients died in those episodes in history. It doesn't look like The Gift-Source was doing any covering and protecting in those instances."

Chaos countered by saying, "Notice your words: It doesn't *look like* He was doing any covering and protecting. The Gift-Source actually was covering and protecting them. Let me show you.

"But let me first ask you something. Would you allow your child to be crucified on a cross to save the world from eternal death? No, you wouldn't! But that is what The Gift-Source did. The Gift-Source allowed His Son to be tortured, tormented and crucified so that people on earth could have the opportunity to receive eternal life. Such a sacrifice would cover your wrongdoings in the past, present and future.

"The Gift-Source allowed His child to be sacrificed so that many could be saved from eternal death. It's hard to believe but it is true. It didn't look like The Gift-Source was covering and protecting. But He was.

"The Gift-Source sacrificed His only Child for the greater good — knowing that some humans would either accept or reject Him and His Son. It looked like all was lost because The Son suffered a terrible death on a cross and eventually died; but He was resurrected from the dead and today He lives. You may not physically be able to see Him but He lives.

"Now back to my original thought.

"First of all, sufferings, sorrows, troubles, ups and downs are part of life's journey. There are times through permissive will, The Gift-Source allows storms and struggles to rage in your life so that He can either get you to where you need to be or to get you back to where you ought to be. The Gift-Source sometimes allows you to experience the down-side of life to strengthen your faith and develop your purpose.

"Think about it like this: Had you not experienced someone betraying your trust for example, you would not be trustworthy today. Had you not known what is to be poor, you would not know how to empathize with those in need. Had you not known what it means to be in an abusive relationship, you would not be able to help others who are experiencing the same thing.

"Secondly, it's actually a win-win situation for The Gift-Source's recipients — man, woman, boy or girl. You see, gift-recipients are guaranteed eternal life. On earth, they are covered but even if they are taken from the earth by way of death, they will go home to live with The Gift-Source in heaven for eternity where there is no more sickness, death, wickedness, or any heartache. I'm not allowed in heaven either.

"In heaven, there is rest, peace, joy, and life-everlasting. So, it's a win-win. Sure it hurts to see loved ones go but would you rather see them suffer on earth or live eternally in peace?

"Here's another one. You mentioned 911. The Gift-Source did not cause the tragedy on September 11, 2001 with planes crashing into New York City's World Trade Center towers. But through His permissive will, The Gift-Source allowed it to happen. I am convinced that whenever a gift-recipient is in trouble, The Gift-Source does one of two things. He will either snatch the recipient out of harm's way or get in the trouble with the recipient and carry them through it.

"Oh, you do know that The Gift-Source was in the fire with His recipients on September 11, 2001, don't you? The fire was heated hotter than a normal fire because of the jet fuel. The Gift-Source's recipients were tied and bound by the seat belts of the planes. Keep on looking. Those who carried them to the furnace died also.

"If you stop now, you will stop too early and miss The Gift-Source's Son. He was there too. How do we know He was there? Because He left evidence. In the remains of the tragedy, the searchers found a cross intact! What does the cross mean? The cross means victory. The cross means life. The cross means power over physical death. The cross represents the presence of The Son.

"So I repeat. The Son was there at the World Trade Center on September 11, 2001.

How do we know He was there? Because He left evidence.

"Sometimes The Gift-Source's actions don't make logical sense. But you have to understand that what you go through, ultimately works out for a greater good. It may take a long time for deliverance. And if you don't get delivered, The Gift-Source will keep (take care of) you in the process to help you endure.

"Now, back to my original point for this lesson," said Chaos.

"When gift-recipients totally disregard The Gift-Source, that's when I can use one of my other aliases, like Pandemonium. If I can negatively affect gift-recipients, they will get weak, lost and in some cases, violent. That's when my originator is most pleased.

"Someone drew a cartoon once that illustrated the aftermath of a high school shooting spree and there were two characters in the drawing who were talking about The Gift-Source who knows all, sees all and is all-powerful.

"One of the characters asked the question, 'Why didn't The Gift-Source prevent the shooting?'

"The other character said, 'How could He prevent it? The Gift-Source is not allowed in school anymore.'

"And there it is. The Gift-Source is the answer to your problems with me. You ask the question, 'What is the solution to all the chaos in your life, the world or life in general?' The answer is The Gift-Source.

"Now the next question you should ask The Gift-Source is not 'Why all the chaos?'

"No, the next question you should ask is, 'What can I learn from the chaos?'

"It's also important to remember that if you do not have a relationship with The Gift-Source, you might not get the right answers you need. That is why The Son was sent so that you could connect with The Gift-Source. With that relationship-connection, you have access to what you need.

"Let me say that another way. The Gift-Source has the answers you need but you have to let The Gift-Source have access to your heart. He sent The Son on His behalf to be with you and to give you a chance to receive eternal life. However, The Son will not come into your life if you don't accept Him.

"Some won't even allow The Gift-Source into their own homes. Let me take that a step further. When was the last time you talked to The Gift-Source with your children? Have things like money, prestige, so-called status, social media accounts, and all the latest technology gadgets replaced quality time with your children? If you are not careful, you too could have the beginnings of a gift-recipient prone to do horrible things. And then you'll wonder, 'Where did I go wrong?'

"Let's take it another step further. The Gift-Source is also a Divine Influencer. However, some will not let The Gift-Source be the Divine Influencer over their individual life. If The Gift-Source is not the Divine Influencer of one's life, how do they expect their children to be divinely influenced?"

"What are you talking about?," asked Human.

"Let me illustrate," said Chaos. "The orator and abolitionist, Frederick Douglas, once said that it is easier to build children than it is to repair a broken man."

Chaos elaborated on his message more. "Maybe you and other gift-recipients should ask yourselves, "What kind of behavior do I demonstrate in front of my children? Who do I worship? What philosophies do I identify with? What are my habits? What do my children see me doing? On who or what do my children see me focusing my affections?

"Why do you think some children are rebellious? Could it be that they inherited their parents' rebellious spirit?

"You may say, 'Well, I sent my children to The Gift-Source's house for teaching and training.'

"Yes, that may be true but did you go with them? Did you continue to train them when they came home? When you don't go to be trained and taught, that is sending them a message too. If they don't see you attending, then they will grow up to think, The Gift-Source's training and teaching are not important for them either until there is a crisis.

THE SEED REVELATION

"Before I take my exit and another unexpected gift shows up, let me talk with you about the seed revelation. Seeds produce fruit. Likewise, your spiritual seeds produce spiritual fruit. Your spiritual fruit are life qualities you exhibit.

"Do you exhibit quality spiritual fruit found in the Book: Love, joy, peace, patience, kindness, goodness, faithfulness, gentleness and self-control?

"Or do you prefer to exhibit immoral fruit like sexual immorality, impurity and corruption; idolatry and witchcraft; hatred, discord, jealousy, fits of rage, selfish ambition, dissensions, divisions, envy, drunkenness, orgies, and the like? I personally prefer this group because they work well in the situations I create," said Chaos.

"But don't you get too holy. The Gift-Source is able to save, deliver and change anyone for the good; and that includes those who produce immoral fruit. He can change their immoral lifestyle to one which produces quality spiritual fruit.

"Like a farmer's seed, your quality spiritual fruit is guaranteed if you allow your personal seed to fall to the ground and die so that it can produce more quality fruit.

"The results are locked in. The spiritual genetic formula for tearing down strongholds, destroying principalities, casting out demons and taking back what my originator stole from you is already sealed inside quality seeds. When you submit to The Gift-Source's authority, your seeds grow because you are covered by The Gift-Source's Son and you follow The Guidance Counselor's advice.

"The danger is, if obedience does not take place, you may find yourself functioning — without Guidance-Counselor's special power called the anointing.

"If there is no joy, no peace... if your position is a continuous source of pain, check out your anointing. If any recipient operates their gift (created purpose) outside the scope of authority delegated to them, then the gift loses its anointing and that recipient no longer has authority over anything.

"The expansion of your gift upon your authority is how you handle that which has been given to you. To be in authority, you must be under authority. If you leave your delegated area or if you are disobedient to the delegated leadership, your authority is revoked."

CONFLICT VS. GIFT

"A movement from me, Chaos, toward discipline requires a special word of truth, knowledge and wisdom, delivered from The Gift-Source to your mind. This special word is known as revelation. As revelations are shared over your internal, spiritual 'inner-net,' your response is critical; for the Book says, you must not be a hearer only but a doer as well. Meaning, do not merely listen to or read the Book, and so deceive yourself. Do what it says.

"Focus on discipleship. A disciple is a disciplined one. In a word, that is initial positive contact with The Son. However, the goal is to make disciples. As gift-recipients, you are not ready-made disciples. You only have the potential. The question goes out: 'How do you know if you are a disciplined one?'

"The word, 'disciple,' carries the idea of four things. I have a list here of those items and it reads like this: 'A disciple is one who does:
     Number one, what ought to be done.
     Number two, what needs to be done, when it should be done.
     Number three, what needs to be done, when it should be done as well as it

can be done.

Number four, all of the above every time they need to be done.'

"That's a disciplined one. Are you with me?

"If revelation of truth is essential for discipline, then my originator's chief weapon must be deception. Spiritual maturity, through discipline is largely dependent upon revelation. My originator's war games rest upon lies, half-truths, manipulation, illusion, delusion, schemes and deception.

"I am convinced that gift-recipients are in daily need of deliverance, discipline and development. First, you need deliverance from things and circumstances that distract you. Secondly, you need discipline in your behavior. Thirdly, you must develop in your personal area of delegated authority, in order for you to live a life on purpose and power.

"As I inspect the fruit of many gift-recipients, the struggle is my originator has tricked so many into non-essential battles.

"Once you have made contact with truth and your movement is directed and empowered through the Guidance-Counselor, discipline is the result. Your relationship with truth and revelation of truth, triggers a spiritual walk whereby superficial, deceptive and manipulative tools no longer disease your belief system. Consistency is the word of choice. Character and integrity are the fruit."

CONTACT WITH THE SON

"The Gift-Source so loved the world, that He gave His only Son Who sacrificed Himself to save the world and whoever believes in The Son shall not perish, but have eternal, everlasting life.

"If you want eternal life, you must have contact with and believe in The Son. When you believe in The Son, The Gift-Source adopts you as His child too. Then you can say, 'I know who I am. I know whose I am and I know what I am. In a word, I know that my initial positive contact with The Son, based on the revelation of truth, places me into the family of The Gift-Source. It is because of The Gift-Source that I move and have my being.'

"You are a disciplined gift-recipient in the process of maturing. Now that you qualify for service, what shall you do? What is your purpose?'

"But I know all this already," said Human, "because I accepted The Son and I know that I am also a child of The Gift-Source. What's your point here?"

"Clearing its throat, Chaos apologized saying, "Oh yes. Excuse me. I digressed again," and continued with the lesson.

"The question is critical. It is one of life's toughest questions with all of the mean, dysfunctional relationships, frustration, confusion and chaos. You ask, 'Why am I here?'

"For even the strongest gift-recipient, life seems at times, useless, tiresome, unfulfilling, insignificant and uncontrollable. I am convinced that life begins with The Son at the center.

"There are so many gift-recipients who are depressed, frustrated, addicted to substitutes and sidetracked by attractive alternatives because of no contact with The Son. The Book says in one of the chapters that The Son comes so that you and other gift-recipients will have life — but not just have life, but have a fulfilling and abundant life.

"It is important at this moment to understand that you were not created for time, but for eternity. Time only serves as an instrument to allow you space to make a divine choice. Life is really a dress rehearsal for eternity. It is not just the 'here and now' that matters. You need an eternal perspective. You must come to grips with the fact that what you are doing now is preparation for eternal-living or eternal-death.

"The primary purpose of gift-recipients' existence on earth is to glorify The Gift-

Source and secondly, to extend His legacy through a tri-lateral relationship.

> **"Step One:** Establish a quality relationship with The Gift-Source — develop the upper.
> **Step Two:** You must develop yourself to your highest potential — develop the inner.
> **Step Three:** Seek the best good for yourself and others — develop the outer.

"Sometimes The Gift-Source allows you to have certain experiences with me, Chaos, to prepare you for something greater and better. Other times, experiences with me show that you spend valuable time and energy striving for what is not the answer.

"Many gift-recipients have said, '*If* I had a nice home... *If* I had a better job... *If* I were well-known... *If* I had this or that... I would have it all together and be happy. *If* I just had a husband or wife... IF... IF... IF... Stuff and things are not the answer to your problems. The Gift-Source is the answer!"

FINDING TRUE LIFE

"I want to suggest that you often look in the wrong places for what you really need. The struggle is many gift-recipients do not really know that The Gift-Source is all they need until The Gift-Source is all they have.

"You grasp at what you think you want, at what you see, but everything that looks good to you is not good for you. Someone once said, 'Don't lose what you have… trying to get what you don't need.'

"How do you reach that level of purposed living in which you can say and mean it: 'This joy I have, the world didn't give it to me and the world can't take it away'? If your joy, life and purpose are controlled by anything or anyone other than The Gift-Source, inconsistent living will be the result.

"Life's purpose and individual vision connects people to abundant living. Here are three powerful nuggets that if learned and applied, they would give purpose and meaning to your life.

"**Number one,** The Gift-Source knows all and knows how gift-recipients are uniquely created. That's a creative claim and that's why certain gifts are especially designed for you."

Number two, gift-recipients are The Gift-Source's people. That's a redemptive claim.

Number three, gift-recipients are the sheep of The Gift-Source's pasture. That's a directive claim. Yes, The Gift-Source is a Shepherd too Who leads gift-recipients — protecting them, watching over them, and taking care of them."

ORDERED PURPOSE: REALIZING YOUR POTENTIAL

"The Son promised, 'The work that I do, even greater things than this shall you do because I go to My Father, The Gift Source; and whatever you ask in My name, I will do it so that I may bring glory to My Father.'

"Imagine if you will, two great athletes — one, a basketball player and the other, a hockey player. Both are great at applying all their skills and energy toward the opponents' goals. The picture I think is clear. Despite their talents and efforts, if their skills are directed toward the wrong goal, the time spent on the floor playing their respective game would frustrate their purpose for being there.

"Likewise, gift-recipients who participate on the field of life must be clear on some things like what team they are on. Are they on The Gift-Source's team or on my originator, the enemy's team? Furthermore, they must be clear on their assigned gifts, delegated area of authority, and clearly articulated goals.

"In order to fulfill a purpose, you have been dispatched from eternity into time. You are a time capsule carrying a deposit of the essence of The Gift-Source, for release of your good work into this present age.

"Those good works can only be extracted according to order, purpose and planning. So many suffer and meander through life looking for their life's purpose. They often miss the mark in search for the complex when the answer is hidden in the simple.

"Through a developed relationship and committing yourself to The Gift-Source's direction, leading and work, you place yourself on a clear journey. The Gift-Source will provide you with direction through revelation, and therefore, move you from me, Chaos, to discipline and will order your steps."

Chapter 7

THE HOPE OF CHAOS

"New paradigm models come as the result of a growth mandate to change. Let's face it. Sometimes change is uncomfortable. In a word, change brings me, Chaos, into the picture. However, out of me, comes new models for operating and living.

"In your situation, as uncertain as it seems, The Gift-Source is creating new paradigm models all around your painful condition. Are you listening?

"**DO NOT BE UPSET BECAUSE OF ME, CHAOS.** Why not? Because, believe it or not, all things will work together for your good and those who are called according to The Gift-Source's purpose.

"How do I know everything will be alright? Because the Guidance-Counselor's Spirit is alive and bursting out of me, Chaos, with a re-creative order for a new world. You must understand that your assembly here on earth represents a 'cosmic cry.'

"In one of the Book's chapters, there is an account about how the cry of some gift-recipients came up before The Gift-Source. It does not say the 'petition.' It does not say the 'request.' It says 'the cry' which is a literal pleading, came up before The Gift-Source.

"Then according to the Book, The Gift-Source heard their cry. It is not until you cry, that the new model (paradigm) comes bursting out of the chaos. So if you have not cried out, there will be no new model. But when you 'cry' out to The Gift-Source, the new model appears in the middle of the chaos.

"My question to you as you stand against the backdrop of personal chaos, confusion... as you wrestle, not against flesh and blood, but against principalities, against powers, against the rulers of the darkness of this age, what is your perception of The Gift-Source? Think about all the gifts, talents, skills and abilities you have. Also, look at your life. What do you see? Can you clearly see The Gift-Source's created purpose for you?

"Yes, you see me, Chaos, but look again. When you look up, The Gift-Source will restore your sight and give you a different perspective. Then, you will see my value and purpose."

NEVER FORSAKEN

Before Chaos could close out the teaching session, another message arrived with some encouragement.

The message was written by one of Gift Giver's Psalmists and it said: "I was young, and now I am old, but I have never seen The Gift-Source's recipients left helpless or their children begging for what they need."

Human listened even more intently because the message sounded too good to be true.

"In the midst of your chaos, cling to The Gift-Source's faithfulness. The Gift-Source's provisional hand is still working in the worst of times and in the best of times. By His mercies, you have been kept from complete destruction by your own hands and also by the enemy's hands.

"The Gift-Source also promises future restoration and blessings to you. Trusting in The Gift-Source's faithfulness day by day gives you confidence in His great promise for the future.

"The notion of healing begins with the healing of individuals. The Gift-Source willingly responds with help when you ask in faith. Faith is only as good as the object in which it is placed. In your case, you must put your faith in The Gift-Source if you expect to get through me, Chaos.

"As you journey on with the deliverance and healing that is found in this lesson, perhaps there is some wrongdoing or mistakes in your life that you thought were unforgiveable.

"The Gift-Source's steadfast love and mercy are greater than any wrongdoing; and He not only promises forgiveness but restoration as well. Can you feel the power, strength and blessed assurance in the message you just received?

"Look at the message this way: I have been young, [been there, done that], but now I'm old. Yet, never have I seen gift-recipients forsaken nor their descendants begging for what they need. The Gift-Source takes care of gift-recipients and makes sure their needs are met.

"In light of the fact that The Gift-Source is in charge of earth-running and to speak with Him, expecting deliverance, can only take place through The Son and faith directing your journey, allow me some pen time to suggest three final thoughts regarding the faithfulness of The Gift-Source.

"You may want to write these down and keep them in mind if you ever encounter me, Chaos, again. First, The Gift Source is in charge. Secondly, The Gift Source works according to the measure of your faith. Thirdly, The Gift-Source's grace is sufficient."

THE GIFT-SOURCE IS IN CHARGE

"With everything that is going on, not only around you, but in and through you, it is comforting to know that The Gift-Source is in charge. Even if buildings are falling, nations are at war, turmoil is everywhere and Pandemonium is at work, you may rest assured, know that The Gift-Source is in charge. I know it's hard to believe.

"Remember that The Gift-Source is all-powerful, all-knowing, and in every place at the same time. The Gift-Source does not have to look for terrorists. Threats do not move Him. Biological warfare does not frighten Him. For you, this should really be comforting, because without a doubt, The Gift-Source is really in charge.

"If you don't know that The Gift-Source is in charge, then when trouble comes and you are trapped in a situation where no earthly force can help you, you don't know how you're coming out of the trouble. However, once you determine in your being that The Gift-Source is in charge, you know with confidence how you are coming out.

"You don't always know when you are coming out or what you will have to go through before you come out. Every gift-recipient will go through something.

"So, remember, The Gift-Source is with you as you go through trouble or chaos. That means what you are going through is not permanent. What you are going through right now is temporary and you will come out of it. If The Gift-Source is on your side, then all things will work together for your benefit.

"You and other gift-recipients are not in charge. You have stewardship privileges, but you own nothing and you are not in charge of anything. Can I help you get out? Simply because if you (and not The Gift-Source) are in charge or if you don't have The Gift-Source's assistance, then your plans will falter. You do not know enough to keep it up. Whatever a gift-recipient has set up for its ownership and control, it may take a long time, but it will eventually fail. At the risk of sounding redundant, The Gift-Source is in charge."

Human looked in unbelief and with a little disagreement.

"Oh, you don't share my belief? OK, Mr. or Ms. Important, when was the last time, The Gift-Source called you in to discuss the weather? How about the dressing of the seasons? Or the direction of the wind? I know it is painful. It just plain old hurts with all that pumped up pseudo-authority you have, but you are not in charge of anything.

"One day, you step out in the morning and the sun is shining. The Gift-Source did not ask you anything. The weekend is coming and you got plans to take a trip or you just washed the car but suddenly with no warning... no phone call... no e-mail or fax... it just rains.

> **Please understand that the Gift-Source works according to the measure of your faith.**

"When The Gift-Source gets ready to do something, no meeting is called. There is no meeting with your leadership team. The Gift-Source just goes about the business of earth-running. Revisit the message. The Gift-Source's recipients — whether young or old gift-recipients — have never been forsaken nor have their children had to beg for what they need.

"There is pain around the world. You feel alone, but I must tell you that you have not been forsaken, abandoned or betrayed by The Gift-Source. There are times when you feel like nobody knows how rough it is; but if you come and don't hide in your room... come to The Gift-Source's house and listen, you will hear another gift-recipient exclaim, 'That's right! Amen.' The non-verbal gift-recipient will wave a hand.

"What those gift-recipients are really saying is, 'I have been there and The Gift-Source did not forsake me.' If you keep on listening, you will hear them say, there is no secret what The Gift-Source can do.

"If you keep on listening, you will hear them say, "The Gift-Source will provide. The Gift-Source will never let you down, never forsake you."

"So, if you are hurting or standing in fear, help is on the way. The Gift-Source works according to the measure of your faith.

"Everything is possible for the one who has faith.' If that is true, and it is, let me ask you two vital questions: 'What are you expecting The Gift-Source to do *in* your life? What are you expecting The Gift-Source to do *through* your life?'"

"Please understand that The Gift-Source works according to the measure of your faith. Since The Gift-Source has unlimited power, you should not limit that power because of your expectations. You limit the activity of The Gift-Source in your life by your own belief or lack thereof.

"The Gift-Source has given you the key to His storehouse of blessings but you refuse to believe He will honor His promises.

"The question that's giving voice in the halls of my mind is this: 'Is there anything too hard for The Gift-Source?'

"The answer is 'No!' There is no problem too large and there is no request that He cannot handle.

"The Gift-Source can give you a thousand blessings just as easy as giving you one. So then, the issue really becomes your faith. What are you willing to believe The

Gift-Source for? If you want to see The Gift-Source's power operating in your life... if you want to get rid of me, Chaos... you must first believe The Gift-Source in faith.

"You must verbalize your faith. You must announce what you are and believe The Gift-Source is going to honor His promises. You must not just think it in your mind. You must announce it, speak it. You must verbalize it. Come closer. That's what a goal is.

"Hold up. What is faith? Faith is the substance of things hoped for and evidence of things not seen. Faith convinces you that what you cannot see is really there. "A goal is a statement of faith. When you set a goal, you must believe The Gift-Source can help you do it. You can do all things through The Son Who strengthens you. Goals are simply statements of faith.

"The size of your goal is determined by the size of your faith in The Gift-Source. Tell me what your goals are in life and I will tell you what you are believing about The Gift-Source. It is important that you announce your goals up front. Say the goals in faith.

"Your tongue is like the rudder that moves a ship. The way you talk to yourself and to others directs the course of your life. So whatever you say about your life... about your relationships... about your marriage... about your job... about your health... about your finances... about your children are sometimes spoken into existence.

"Many times you are waiting for The Gift-Source to do something and believing Him for a miracle but are short-circuiting it by the way you talk. You are believing on the one hand, but denying it on the other with negative thoughts, talk and complaints." As Chaos continued, a chorus of gift-recipients stood up and shouted.

One gift-recipient said, "I believe The Gift-Source is going to work a miracle in my marriage, but He doesn't have much to work with. I don't see how The Gift-

Source is going to do it."

Another gift-recipient said, "Yes, I am praying that my children take a stand for The Gift-Source but they are hopeless."

"I'm praying that The Gift-Source will heal me, but I'm never going to get well."

"I want The Gift-Source to change my life and help me break these bad habits, but that's just the way I am. I'm never going to change."

"When you think negative like what those gift-recipients just said, you short-circuit The Gift-Source's power in your life; and it's all because of your mouth and thoughts.

"Walk with me. I'm almost done with the lesson. But you have to believe that The Gift-Source is going to work in your favor and turn this chaos around so that things will work out for your good."

THE GIFT-SOURCE'S GRACE IS SUFFICIENT

"You must act in faith. In other words, you must step out in advance before power is released. The Gift-Source wants you to take action even before you feel anything. For example, you must believe and act in confidence as if you have the power and healing... even though it has not officially arrived. That's called acting in faith.

"You step out in advance, before you feel or see anything and your faith moves The Gift-Source. If you only act and pray when you feel like it, the enemy is going to make sure you never feel like it. Immaturity is living by feelings. Maturity is living by commitment.

"Sometimes you say, 'There is something I would really like to do, but I don't think I can.' So you never even try. As a result, you never have power. If you had tried, The Gift-Source would have poured the needed power into your life. If you take one step, He will give you the strength to make the journey."

"The Gift-Source wants to share His power with you but you must start the process. First, admit you have a need. Secondly, believe in faith. Thirdly, speak in faith. And finally, act in faith.

"In other words step out in advance, acting 'as if.' You are waiting for The Gift-Source to do a miracle in your life and think you are waiting on The Gift-Source. In reality, The Gift-Source is waiting on *you* to take that first step. The power will not be released until you take that first step. You must tell yourself at times, 'I don't feel it, but I *know* the faithfulness of The Gift-Source. So, on His Word, I step out on faith. It is the right thing to do.'

"Having faith in The Gift-Source means trusting, believing, relying, depending and obeying. Trust The Gift-Source in the shadows, as well as in the sunshine. Believe The Gift-Source when the going gets tough, as well as when the going is easy. Rely on The Gift-Source through the bad times as well as through the good times. Depend on The Gift-Source when you do not understand something as well as when you do understand. Obey The Gift-Source when other gift-recipients don't, as well as when they do.

"Faith in The Gift-Source also means confiding in The Gift-Source when your cupboard is empty, as well as when it's full. Faith means believing deliverance from sin or deliverance from temptation. Whether it be for strength renewal or health restoration... whether it be for dissolving doubts or removing fear... faith believes that The Gift-Source's... grace is sufficient... mercy is abundant...His Word is accurate... and presence is assuring."

As Chaos began to exit, another unexpected gift showed up on Human's doorstep and introduced itself. "Hello! My name is Struggle!"

To learn more about other "thorn" gifts, including the gift of struggle,
stay tuned for the next installment in the *"The Gift, Your Gift"* series
and visit **tgygift.com** for more information.

Decision Time

Ok. Now it's your time to make a decision. You have heard the chaos. You have seen the chaos. You've experienced the chaos. Are you ready to give up? Do you choose to panic and give in to fear?

In the midst of your chaos, what do you do with what you see? What do you do when you don't know what to do? Or do you see the blessing in disguise that chaos can be? What you decide will reflect what you believe.

No, it's not easy but there is Someone Who can handle it better than you can. You may already know The Gift-Source but then again, you might not. If you don't know The Gift-Source (God the Father) or His Son (Jesus Christ) here's how you can know Him and have eternal life. If you are tired of the chaos, consider His invitation to discipleship and plan of salvation.

The Invitation to Discipleship

John 3:16 (KJV) — *For God so loved the world that He gave His only begotten Son, that whosoever believeth in Him should not perish but have everlasting life.*

Romans 10:9 (KJV) — *That if thou shalt confess with thy mouth the Lord Jesus, and believe in thine heart that God hath raised Him from the dead, thou shalt be saved.*

God's plan for your life is that you come to know Jesus in a more personal way. This is a very simple plan that can be found by following these steps:

STEP 1: Realize that you are a sinner.

Romans 3:23 (KJV) — *For all have sinned and come short of the glory of God.*

STEP 2: Realize that there is a consequence for sin.

Romans 6:23a (KJV) — *For the wages of sin is death...*

STEP 3: Realize that God offers you a free gift.

Romans 6:23b (KJV) — *...but the gift of God is eternal life through Jesus Christ our Lord.*

STEP 4: This step is up to you, whether or not to accept this free gift. It is simple...

Romans 10:9 (KJV) — *That if thou shalt confess with thy mouth the Lord Jesus, and shalt believe in thine heart that God hath raised him from the dead, thou shalt be* *saved.*

If you see your need to receive Jesus Christ as your personal Savior, just pray this simple prayer and you will be saved:

> *"Dear Lord, I know that I am a sinner and need You as my Savior. I believe that You came and died, and rose again for my sins. Please come into my heart and save me from my sins. Amen."*

Dr Ayanna Burns

Ayanna is an aspiring writer and is the Founder/CEO of The Writer's Pensuasion. Through her work, Ayanna seeks to encourage, educate, inspire, and motivate. Since childhood, she has either served or worked in an administrative capacity, most recently at the Beulah Grove Baptist Church (Augusta, GA) for over 26 years (serving as the Church Administrator for the last nine years). Ayanna enjoys reading, writing, solving puzzles and learning. She has also served as a ghost writer for various projects and as an editor of books written by Dr. Sam Davis and Dr. Ralph Watkins (author, minister and professor).

Ayanna received her Doctorate in Business Administration from Argosy University (Atlanta, GA), a Master's in Business Administration from Augusta State University (Augusta, GA), and a Bachelor's in Biology from Augusta College (Augusta, GA).

An avid book reader, she notes, "Some may enjoy shopping for clothes, but I would rather be shopping for books or reading them in a library."

Though not always understanding the reasons why things happen the way they do, Ayanna is a firm believer in the scripture that says all things work together for the good.... (Romans 8:28)

...*The Unexpected Blessings of a Thorn* is her first series of books and marks a new paradigm in her life: Author.

CONTACT INFORMATION
ayanna@twpensuasion.com
Like Ayanna Burns' Author page on Facebook

Dr. Sam Davis

Dr. Sam Davis is married to Mrs. Beverly M. Davis (author of *A Spiritual Walk with God*) and is the pastor of the Beulah Grove Baptist Church (Augusta, GA). He has over 42 years of experience in pastoring, clinical counseling and Christian education. He has a Bachelor of Science degree in Business Administration from Voorhees College (Denmark, South Carolina), a Master of Divinity degree from the Interdenominational Theological Center (Atlanta, Georgia) and a Doctor of Ministry degree specializing in Pastoral/Clinical Counseling from Columbia Theological Seminary (Decatur, Georgia).

Dr. Davis is the author of *When the Multitude Comes: A Guide to Organizing a Growing Church; Strategies to Develop Kingdom Citizens; The New Millennium Deacon; Building Capacity to Build the Kingdom* with Min. Valerie Jackson; and *From a Sheep's Perspective.*

Dr. Davis is the CEO and founder of the 30901 Development Corporation, Inc. (Augusta, GA), Beulah Grove Community Resource Center (Augusta, GA), Kingdom Kids Preparatory School, Lamar Medical Center (Augusta, GA) and Joyful Sound Ministries, Inc. He also help co-found the United Neighborhood Federal Credit Union (Augusta, GA).

NOTES — CHAOS

Preface and Background

2 Corinthians 9

Matthew 19:26

Ephesians 1:5

Philippians 4:19

Romans 8:34; Hebrews 7:25

Romans 8:26-27

John 16:13

Chapter 2

Psalm 30:5

John 10:10

Mark 4:35-40

See Jonah 1:3-15 (NIV)

Chapter 3

Isaiah 43:19

John 13:7

2 Corinthians 5:7

Hebrews 11:6

Chapter 4

Ephesians 3:21

1 Corinthians 2:9

Genesis 3

Chapter 5

Matthew 5:14

Romans 8:38-39

1 John 1:9

Proverbs 18:21

2 Corinthians 5:7

Chapter 6

2 Timothy 3:16-17

Ephesians 6:11-13

John 10:10

Galatians 5:19-23

James 1:22

John 3:16

John 10:10

See Psalm 23

John 14:12

Chapter 7

Romans 8:38

Ephesians 6:12

Psalm 37:25

Romans 8:28, 31

Genesis 22:8; Deuteronomy 31:6, 8

Mark 9:23

Genesis 18:14; Jeremiah 32:27

Hebrews 11:1

Philippians 4:13

See James 3:4-6

Stay tuned as you continue to learn about

Your Gift of other "thorns" in

. . . *The Unexpected Blessings Series of Books* such as:

Chaos

Struggle

Rejectlon

Adversity

Betrayal

Failure

Disappointment

Lack

Hurt

Error

Delay

Loss

Losing

Weakness

Blindness

Deafness

Brokenness

Darkness

Suffering

Setback

The Thorn of _____

(You fill in the blank. What was or is your Thorn
that turned out to be a blessing in disguise?)

ABOUT THE SERIES:

The Gift *Your Gift*

The Unexpected Blessings of...

Matthew 22:1 (AMP) — *AND AGAIN Jesus spoke to them in parables (comparisons, stories used to illustrate and explain)... saying...*

Mark 4:2 (NLT) — *He taught them by telling many stories in the form of parables, such as this one:*

"The Gift, Your Gift" series of books are a collection of modern day allegories and parables. These books were written to do a few things:

1. **To highlight** some of life's most frustrating, difficult issues (i.e, thorns).
2. **To illustrate** how those issues which seem to be to your disadvantage can actually be to your advantage.
3. **To show** that the Bible is just as relevant today as it was thousands of years go.

Most of the books in this series are short reads and some are a little more in depth depending on the subject matter. In each book, God is "The Gift-Source;" His Holy Spirit is "The Guidance Counselor" and His Son, Jesus, is "The Son."

As authors, our intent is to make sure the parables in these books are plain, practical and portable. In other words, they should be clear for you to understand, applicable, and usable wherever you may find yourself in life.

So we hope you are encouraged and inspired knowing that even in chaos, things will eventually work out for your best good.

—Ayanna

FEEDBACK REQUEST

Please visit **tgygift.com** and leave a review of this book or let us know how the book can be improved. If for some reason you did not enjoy the book, then let us know that, too. Your feedback is greatly appreciated as constructive critique is good for the writer's soul!

www.ingramcontent.com/pod-product-compliance
Lightning Source LLC
Chambersburg PA
CBHW070643130626
46555CB00006B/2678